MYSTERY
of the
MISSING FUZZY

Written by Ski Michaels
Illustrated by Dick Smolinski

Troll Associates

Library of Congress Cataloging in Publication Data

Mystery of the missing fuzzy.

Summary: After Fuzzy the caterpillar alarms his
good friends by disappearing one day, they discover
that a friend can change but still be nice.
    [1. Caterpillars—Fiction. 2. Insects—Fiction.
3. Friendship—Fiction. 4. Mystery and detective
stories] I. Smolinski, Dick, ill. II. Title.
PZ7.P3656My   1986   [E]   85-14084
ISBN 0-8167-0646-8 (lib. bdg.)
ISBN 0-8167-0647-6 (pbk.)

Copyright © 1986 by Troll Communications L.L.C.

Published by Troll Associates, an imprint and registered trademark of Troll Communications L.L.C.

Printed in the United States of America.

10   9   8   7   6   5   4   3   2

MYSTERY
of the
MISSING FUZZY

Do you have friends? Friends
are nice to have. Fuzzy
Caterpillar was a good friend.
He was friends with all the bugs
in the garden.

Fuzzy was friends with Ladybug.
Ladybug lived by the flowers in
the garden. Ladybug and Fuzzy
played in the flowers.

Fuzzy was friends with
Grasshopper. Grasshopper lived
in the garden. He lived in the
grass. Together Grasshopper and
Fuzzy had fun eating grass.

Fuzzy was friends with Beetle. Beetle lived in the garden, too. He lived by the big tree. Fuzzy and Beetle went up and down the big tree. Oh, what fun!

Everyone liked Fuzzy. They
liked him just the way he was.
"Don't change," said Ladybug to
Fuzzy.
"Stay the way you are," said
Grasshopper.
"Always be yourself," said
Beetle.

"What good friends!" said
Fuzzy. "I like living in the
garden. I will never go away."

10

But one day, something strange
happened. No one saw Fuzzy.
He was missing. Where was
Fuzzy?

Ladybug missed Fuzzy. She
looked for her friend. Fuzzy was
not playing in the flowers.
"What happened to Fuzzy?"
asked Ladybug.

Grasshopper did not see Fuzzy.
He looked and looked for the
caterpillar.
"Fuzzy usually likes to eat
grass," said Grasshopper.
"Now he is gone. This is very
strange."

Beetle looked for Fuzzy. He
went up and down the big tree.
Beetle saw something strange.
But he did not see Fuzzy.
"What is going on?" said Beetle.

14

Beetle went to see Grasshopper.
"Fuzzy is gone," said Beetle.
Grasshopper said, "He has been
missing for days. I am worried
about Fuzzy."

Beetle and Grasshopper went to
Ladybug.
"Fuzzy is not in the flowers,"
said Beetle. "He is not in the
grass. He is not by the tree.
Fuzzy Caterpillar is not in the
garden."

Ladybug looked worried.
"Fuzzy liked the garden," she
said. "He said he would never go
away. This is a mystery!"

"This mystery must be solved," said Beetle. "But who can solve it?"

"Who?" said Ladybug. "Who can solve the mystery of the missing Fuzzy? Inspector Ant can!"

"Inspector Ant?" said Beetle.
"Who is he?"
"He is a solver of mysteries," said
Ladybug. "Inspector Ant will
find Fuzzy."

The bugs went to see
Inspector Ant.
"We are worried," said
Ladybug.
"Fuzzy Caterpillar is missing,"
said Grasshopper.
"Can you find our friend?" asked
Beetle.

Inspector Ant nodded.
"I will solve the case," said the
Inspector. "I will go to the
garden. I will inspect things.
I will look for clues."

Inspector Ant went to the garden. He looked and inspected. He inspected and looked.
"What a nice garden," he said.
"What a strange mystery."

For days the Inspector looked for
clues. Could he solve the
mystery? Where was Fuzzy?
Inspector Ant went to
Grasshopper.
"Where did you last see Fuzzy?"
he asked.
Grasshopper thought. He
thought about his missing friend.

Grasshopper said, "I saw him in the grass. Fuzzy was eating. He was eating lots and lots of grass." Inspector Ant nodded.
"That is a clue," he said.

Next Inspector Ant went to the big tree. He went to see Beetle.

"Have you seen Fuzzy in the tree today?" asked the Inspector. "No," said Beetle. "But I saw something strange the other day. There is something strange in the tree."

Up the tree went Beetle. Up
went Inspector Ant.
"The strange thing is not the
same," said Beetle. "It has
changed. It was closed the first
time I saw it. Now it is open."

Inspector Ant looked closely at the strange thing. He nodded. "This is a clue," said the Inspector.
Down the tree he went. Down went Beetle, too.

Inspector Ant went to the
flowers. Grasshopper was there.
Beetle was there. Ladybug was
there, too.

Grasshopper was hopping up
and down. Beetle looked
worried. And Ladybug was
yelling.
"Inspector! Inspector!" she
called. "I saw something
strange."

"What did you see?" asked the
Inspector.
"She saw a strange bug," said
Grasshopper.
"It was a funny-looking bug,"
said Beetle.
"It was in the flowers," said
Ladybug.

"Where is the funny bug?" asked
the Inspector.
"You missed it," said Ladybug.
"It flew away."

Inspector Ant nodded.
"A flying bug," said he. "It is
a clue. It is a very good clue.
I think I know where Fuzzy is."

Away went Inspector Ant. The
friends looked at each other.
Was the mystery solved?
Where was Fuzzy?

The next day was the big day.
Inspector Ant called all the bugs
together.
"The case is solved," said the
Inspector. "This is what
happened."

Ladybug looked at Inspector
Ant. Beetle and Grasshopper
looked, too.
"Fuzzy ate a lot of grass," said
Inspector Ant. "Caterpillars eat
a lot when they are going to
change."

"Fuzzy would not change,"
thought Ladybug.
"Friends always stay the same,"
thought Grasshopper.
"Fuzzy will always be Fuzzy,"
thought Beetle.

Inspector Ant went on.
"Fuzzy went up the big tree,"
said he. "Fuzzy made a special
home to go into before he
changed. That was the strange-
looking thing we saw up in the
tree."

"But Fuzzy was not in there
when we looked," said Beetle.
Inspector Ant nodded.
"Then where is Fuzzy?" asked
Ladybug.

"He is up there!" said the
Inspector.
The bugs looked up. There was
the strange bug. The strange bug
was on a flower. It flew down to
the grass.

"Fuzzy Caterpillar is gone," said
Inspector Ant. "But Fuzzy
Butterfly is here. This is Fuzzy!
He is a butterfly now."

"That is not Fuzzy," said
Ladybug.
"He does not look the same,"
said Beetle.
Grasshopper hopped up and
down.
"The mystery is not solved!" he
said.

"It is," said the butterfly. "I am
Fuzzy. I am still your friend. My
looks have changed. But *I* have
not changed."

The butterfly looked at
Ladybug.
"I still like to play in the
flowers," he said.

The butterfly went up to Beetle. "We can go up and down the big tree," he said. "It will be fun."

Grasshopper looked at the
butterfly.
"Do you still eat grass?" he
asked.
"No," said the butterfly. "But I
like grass. We can play in the
grass."

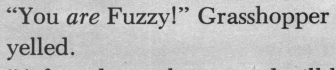

"You *are* Fuzzy!" Grasshopper
yelled.
"A friend can change and still be
nice," said Ladybug.
"We like you the way you are,"
said Beetle.

"What good friends," said Fuzzy
Butterfly. "I like living in the
garden. I will never go away."
"Hooray!" said Fuzzy's friends.

"Case closed," said Inspector Ant.
"The mystery is solved!"